MOBY DICK

ORCHARD BOOKS

Herman Melville
1819 — 1891
who wrote
Moby Dick
and published it in
1851

Here is the whaling ship Pequod...
built for the hunt, with everything
stowed...small boats for the chase...
enough food for three years.

Now her sails are set, and the anchor is weighed.
Bound from Nantucket on a trip round the world...

Come along with ye!

What's to be will be....

Goodbye, and good luck to ye all

On we sailed, past icebergs
and south to warmer seas.

The Chart.

A
CHART
of
the
INDIAN
OCEAN

seychelle ground

The winds blew, the globe turned on...and on...
Then one day (off the Cape of Good Hope)
a sail loomed ahead – a Nantucket whaler
bound for home. A wild sight it was!

Ahoy there! This is
the Pequod bound
round the world!

Have ye seen the
white Whale?
Have ye seen
Moby Dick?

The Albatross

But no reply came, and then as we passed, the shoals of small harmless fish that had been swimming by our side for days darted away to follow the ship Albatross on her lonely way home.

There she blows!

And from then on, every night in the silvery silence, the look-out on the mast saw a ghostly whale-spout far ahead...could this be Moby Dick?

The days and weeks and months rolled on, a thousand leagues of blue, but still not one of us spotted Moby Dick.

With a fair, fresh wind by day we hunted other whales.

At last Mr Flask on Dagoo's shoulders spied a whale...

There she blows!

Stubb kills a whale

Lower away!

Pull up lads!

...and then the dead whale's body was cut up.
Fires were lit on board, and the blubbery skin was boiled for its oil.
Bones and teeth were sorted and stored.

a dead whale is flagged

Cutting - in

lighting the tryworks furnace

Away ye sharks!

the smell is horrible to inhale

cutting-in...the whale is skinned...

Pulling whales' teeth

bundle of whalebone

So weeks and months passed by on the magnificent, mysterious sea...

...and all the time Captain Ahab had only one thought in his head...

He made the harpooneers swear a vow.

And then we all knew we were hunting not just for whales, we were only after the one great, terrible and mysterious white whale Moby Dick. And this filled us all with fear.

So much fear that even the brave Queequeg built a coffin for himself!

Thunder clouds swept by, and the Pacific winds raged... we passed a ship, the Rachel.

And then one calm day we woke to the sound of Captain Ahab hoisting himself one-legged up the main mast.

There she blows! There she blows! A hump like a snowhill - it's Moby Dick!

The Chase
the first day

The men on deck rushed to the rigging to see
the famous whale they had so long been pursuing.

With a great shout the whaleboats were lowered. We rowed like madmen, and Moby Dick burst into view. Taking Captain Ahab's boat in his gigantic white jaws he chopped it clean in two with one awful, splintering crunch.

The Chase
the second day

On the second day Moby Dick rose again. This time the captain's harpoon stuck fast in the whale's side, but in the frenzy of the fight Ahab's whalebone leg was smashed to pieces.

That night the carpenter made Ahab another leg from the broken keel of his wrecked boat.

And on the third day, in a
huge whirlpool of destruction
Moby Dick crashed to the
surface and turned one angry
eye upon us all...

...twisting his vast body in
the water he faced us all..
and charged...

...snapping his jaws amid fiery showers
of foam. His eye then rolled towards
our mother ship, the Pequod...

...from our places amid the chaos
and debris we watched in horror
as the monster whale swam towards
the ship, crashing and lunging,
moving as if he held all the powers
of nature within him, until
his huge, white head smashed
into the shuddering ship which
began at once to sink.

And Captain Ahab, caught round
the neck by his own harpoon rope,
was dragged down to his death
by Moby Dick who disappeared
into the deep.

The sharks! The sharks!

...all was lost...lost in a vast, fizzing,
bubbling, boiling whirlpool of wreckage...

...the ship...the crew...round and round,
down and down...a whirlpool drawing
me ever closer to its black centre.

PEQUOD

Then slowly the sea grew silent until,
rising in a great bubble to the surface
from the sunken ship, Queequeg's empty
coffin shot lengthwise from the water,
fell over, and floated by my side.

The great shroud of the sea rolled on,
as it rolled five thousand years ago...

...and I, alone, am escaped to tell the tale.

The Story of Moby Dick

Sea Raven

Sperm Whales

I have always loved the sea, and as a child my earliest drawings were of old sailing ships, or of divers wrestling underwater with giant octopus and ferocious sharks. I loved to fill my paintings with every kind of sea creature or boat that I could imagine, but my favourite subject was the whale-hunt. I would draw small boats crammed full of little men hurling their tiny harpoons at a mighty, spouting whale.

Back then I did not know why whales were hunted, and it was only when I was older and read the story of Moby Dick that I understood why men chose to sail away on the dangerous and hair-raising hunt for the whale.

The story of Moby Dick is one of the greatest sea stories ever written, and was published more than 100 years ago by Herman Melville who, in his adventures as a young man, actually sailed on an American whaling ship. Melville loved the sea, and Moby Dick is a huge, fantastic book full of wonder at the power and beauty of the ocean and its creatures, especially the whale.

Man has hunted whales since the stone age, but when Melville was writing whaling had become a huge industry. Tens of thousands of whales were killed every year, and whaling ships sailed in their hundreds from ports in America, Britain, Europe and Japan.

At that time products made from whales played a very important part in everyday life. The whale oil – boiled from the whales' blubbery skin – was used in lamps to light homes, streets, and factories. The finest oil – taken from the heads of sperm whales – was taken to make machinery, steam engines (and even pocket watches) run smoothly.

Réunion Island

whale boat

lamp oil

buttons

in the home

street light

Almost every part of the whale, including its bones and teeth, was used to make a huge variety of things such as candles, margarine, pet food, piano keys, umbrellas, clothes, tennis rackets, toys and make-up.

In those days – before oil was drilled from the ground – modern life really did depend on the hunting of whales. As a result, whales no longer lived undisturbed in the safety of the world's vast oceans. They were hunted by men greedy for profit.

The people who sailed on whaling ships were incredibly brave and hardy. Their dangerous journeys would usually last years rather than months, and often involved completing a voyage around the world. Because of this, crew members often came from many different countries. Sometimes a captain would sail with his wife and children. Young boys like Pip were often employed doing some of the hardest and most dangerous jobs.

When Melville wrote Moby Dick most people believed that all creatures were created for man to use and kill as he wished. Nobody seemed to care about the terrible killing of these helpless creatures.

Sadly the slaughter has continued into this century and millions of whales have now disappeared from our oceans. They are now under threat more than ever from man, for even though we no longer depend on whale products, whales are still being hunted today for their oil and blubber. The seas today are busier with ships, and so are more polluted than ever.

In Herman Melville's book Moby Dick I discovered a wonderful celebration of the beauty of the ocean and the amazing skill of man. He has given us a fantastic picture of the nature and power of the sea and of whales. Understanding the history of whaling will help us to preserve the whales that are left, and I am sure you hope as I do that the mysterious ocean will always remain the home of the mighty whale.

AD

dog food

crayons

explosives

My grateful thanks are due to
Sir and Lady Tom and Annie Lucas
for the use of their attic at
Sherman's Hall, Dedham

Thanks also to Francesca Dow and
Frances foster for their enthusiasm
and encouragement

Thank you, too, to James Dodds,
Bob Pyett and Penelope Bray
for their help with whaling reference

This book is dedicated
to my wife
GAYE

ORCHARD BOOKS
96 Leonard Street, London EC2A 4RH
Orchard Books, Australia
14 Mars Road, Lane Cove, NSW 2066
© Allan Drummond 1997
ISBN 1 86039 160 5(hardback)
ISBN 1 86039 914 2 (paperback)
First published in Great Britain in 1997
First published in paperback in 1998
The rights of Allan Drummond to be identified as the author
and illustrator of this Work have been asserted by him in
accordance with the Copyright, Designs and Patents Act 1998.
A CIP catalogue record of this book is available
from the British Library
Printed in Singapore